THOUSAND OAKS LIBRARY

JUN 2004

DISCARDED

THOUSAND OAKS LIBRARY
1401 E. Janss Road
Thousand Oaks, CA 91362

All in One Hour

All in One Hour

Words by
Susan Stevens Crummel

Concept and Pictures by Dorothy Donohue

Marshall Cavendish
New York

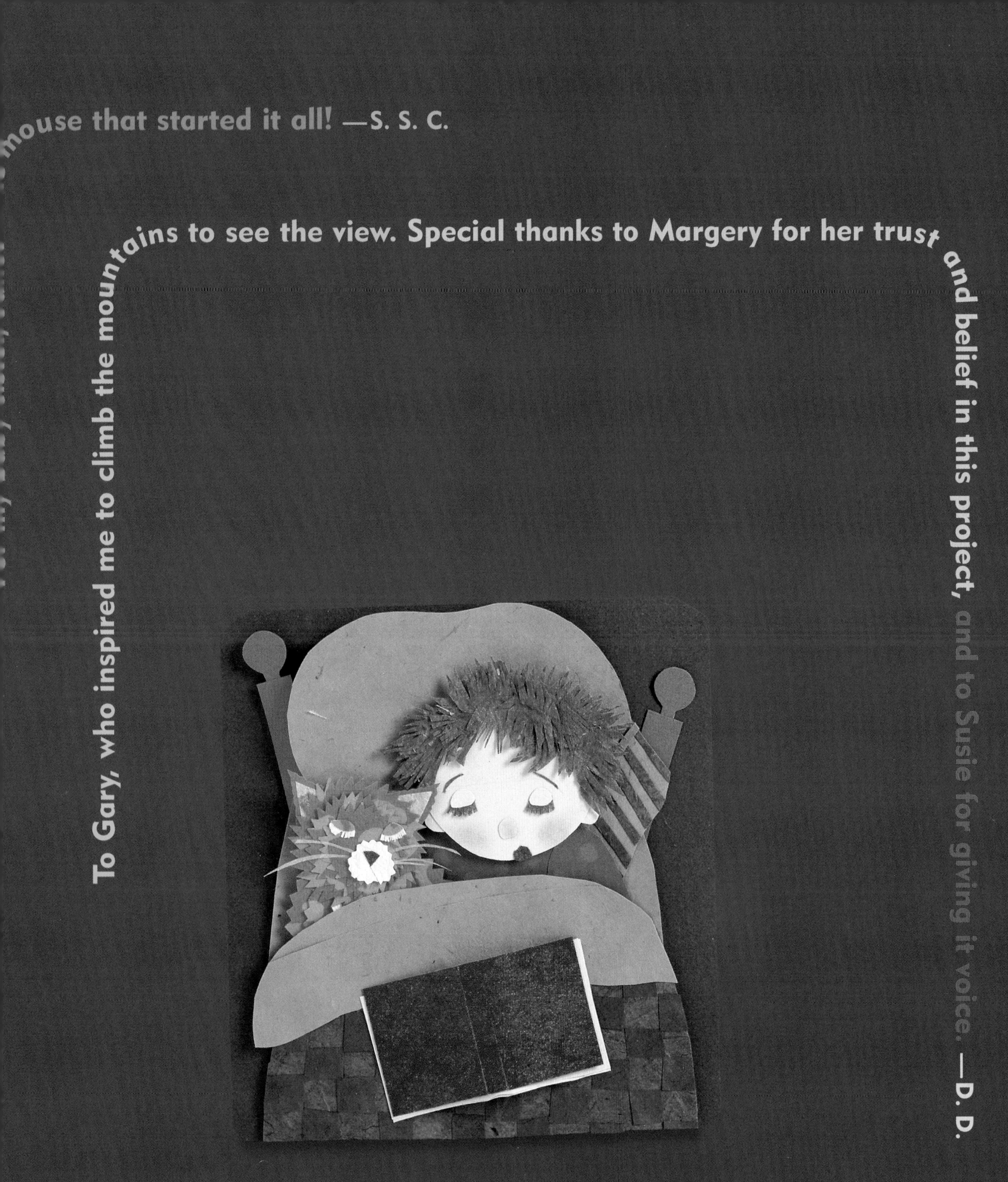

mouse that started it all! —S. S. C.

To Gary, who inspired me to climb the mountains to see the view. Special thanks to Margery for her trust and belief in this project, and to Susie for giving it voice. —D. D.

6:00 A.M. This is the mouse that started it all.

6:02
This is the cat. What happens now? She sees the mouse.
Meow, meow!

6:05 She chases the mouse that started it all.

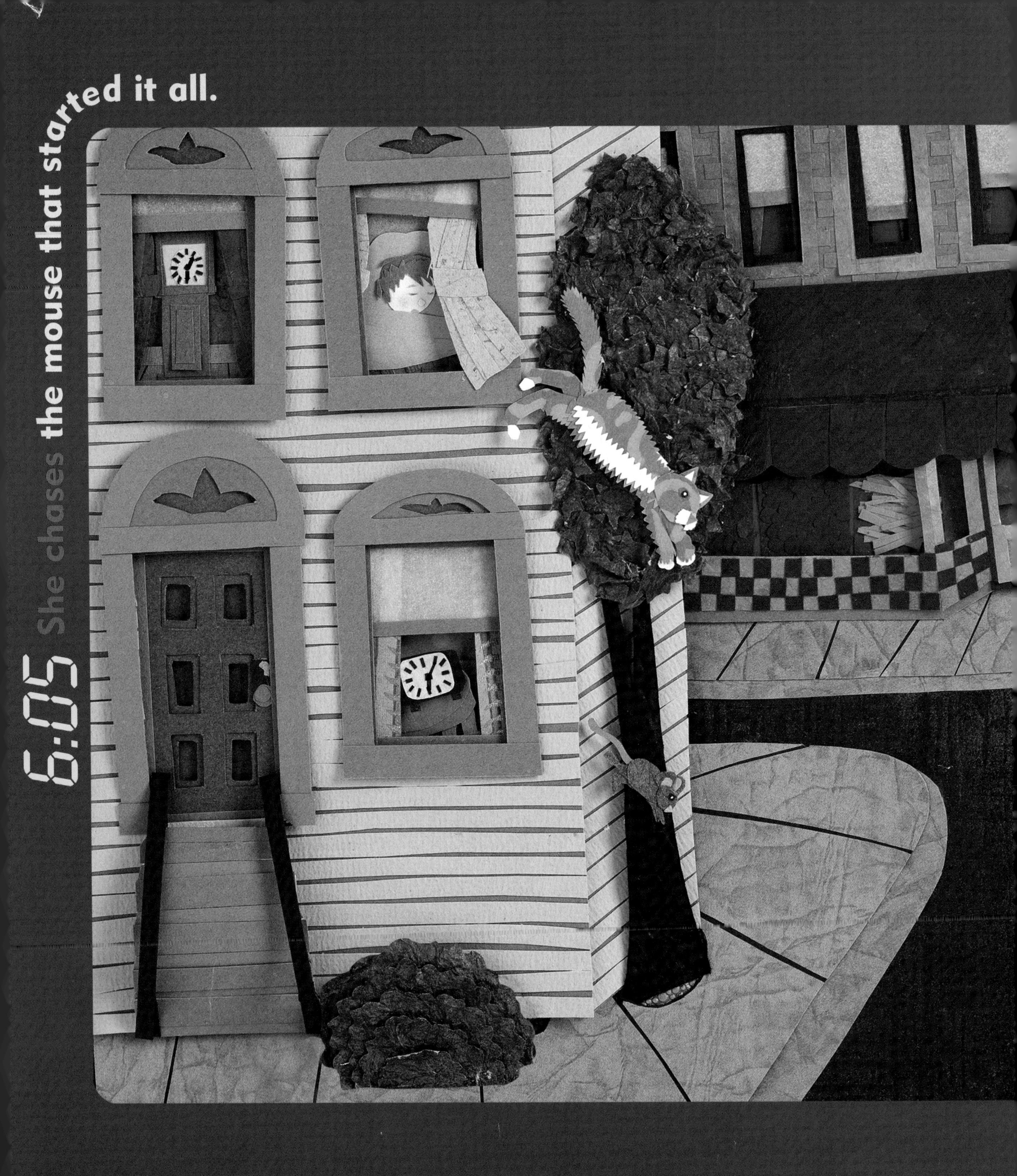

BANK

6:09 This is the dog. What happens now? He sees the cat.
Bow-wow!

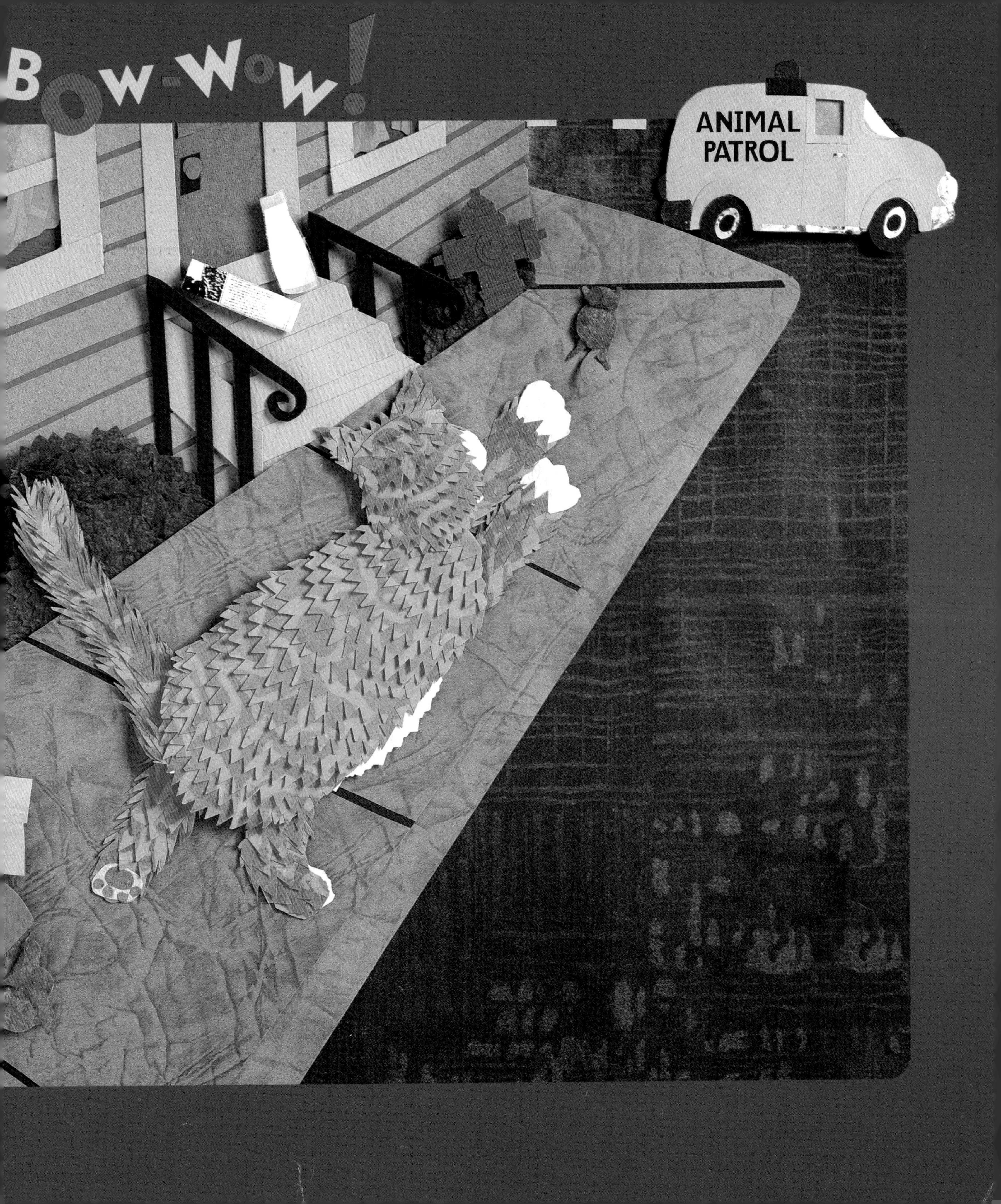
BOW-WOW!
ANIMAL
PATROL

6:11 He chases the cat that chases **the mouse that started it all.**

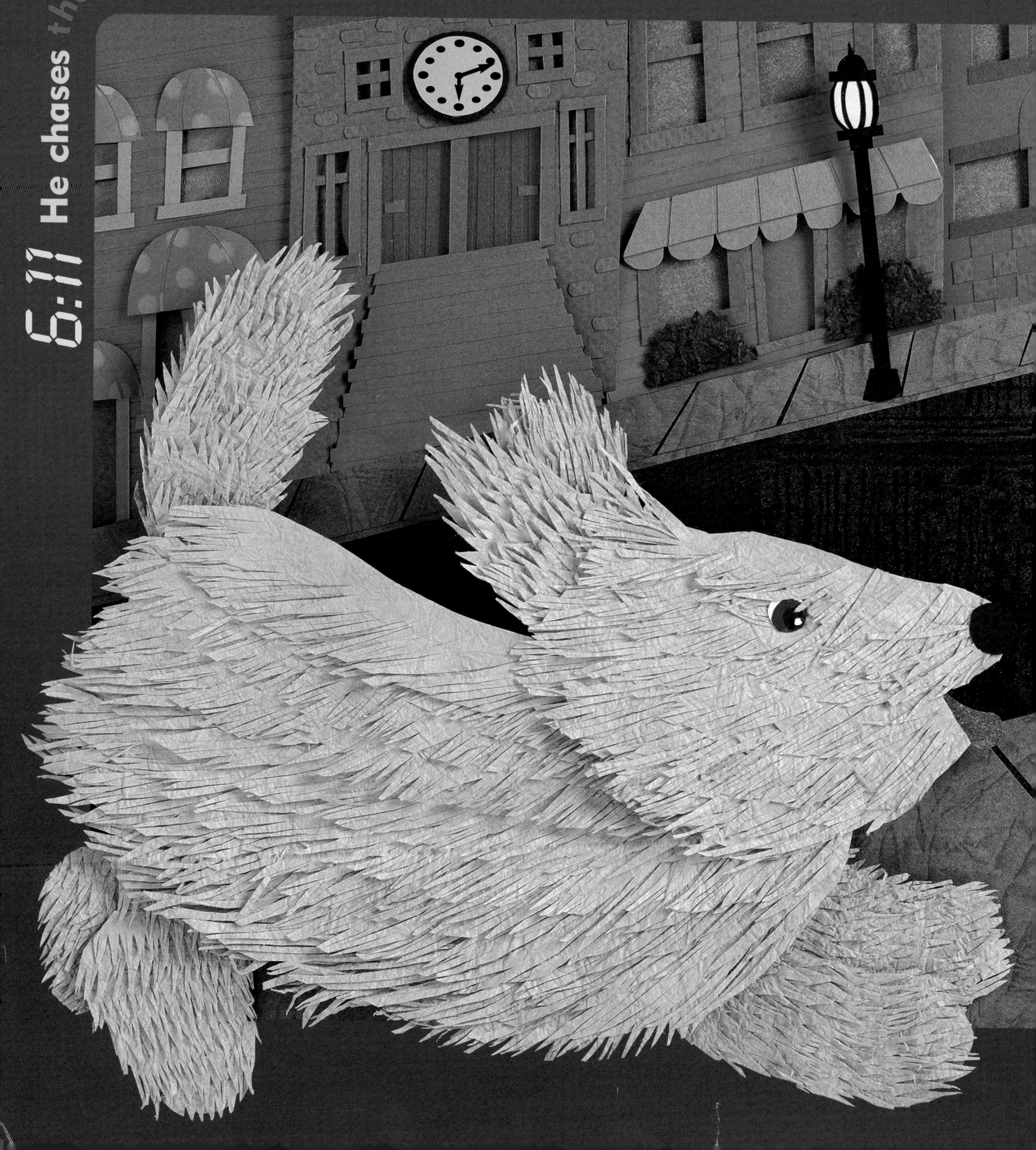

ANIMAL
PATROL
STOP

6:15 This is the dogcatcher. What does she see? The shaggy

brown dog that's out running free. She chases the dog that chases the cat that chases the mouse that started it all.

6:18 This is the robber. What does he get? The cash

from the bank, but it falls in the net.

6:21 He chases the catcher who chases the

dog that chases the cat that chases the mouse that started it all.

6:25
This is the policeman.

What does he hear? The robber who's yelling, "Come here, come here, come here!"

6:29 He chases the

robber who chases the catcher who chases the dog that chases the cat that chases the mouse that started it all.

6:33 **Running so**

fast. Why can't they see? Something might happen. What can it be?

6:37
One minute chasing at each other's heels, next minute slipping on all of those peels!

6:39 Everyone flying up high in the air.

6:44 Everyone **landing** with food everywhere.

6:50 Sort it *all* out. Who goes with whom?

6:55 Back to their places. Back to the room.

7:00 A.M. Back into bed, so sleepy, and then . . .

time to wake up. No, not again!

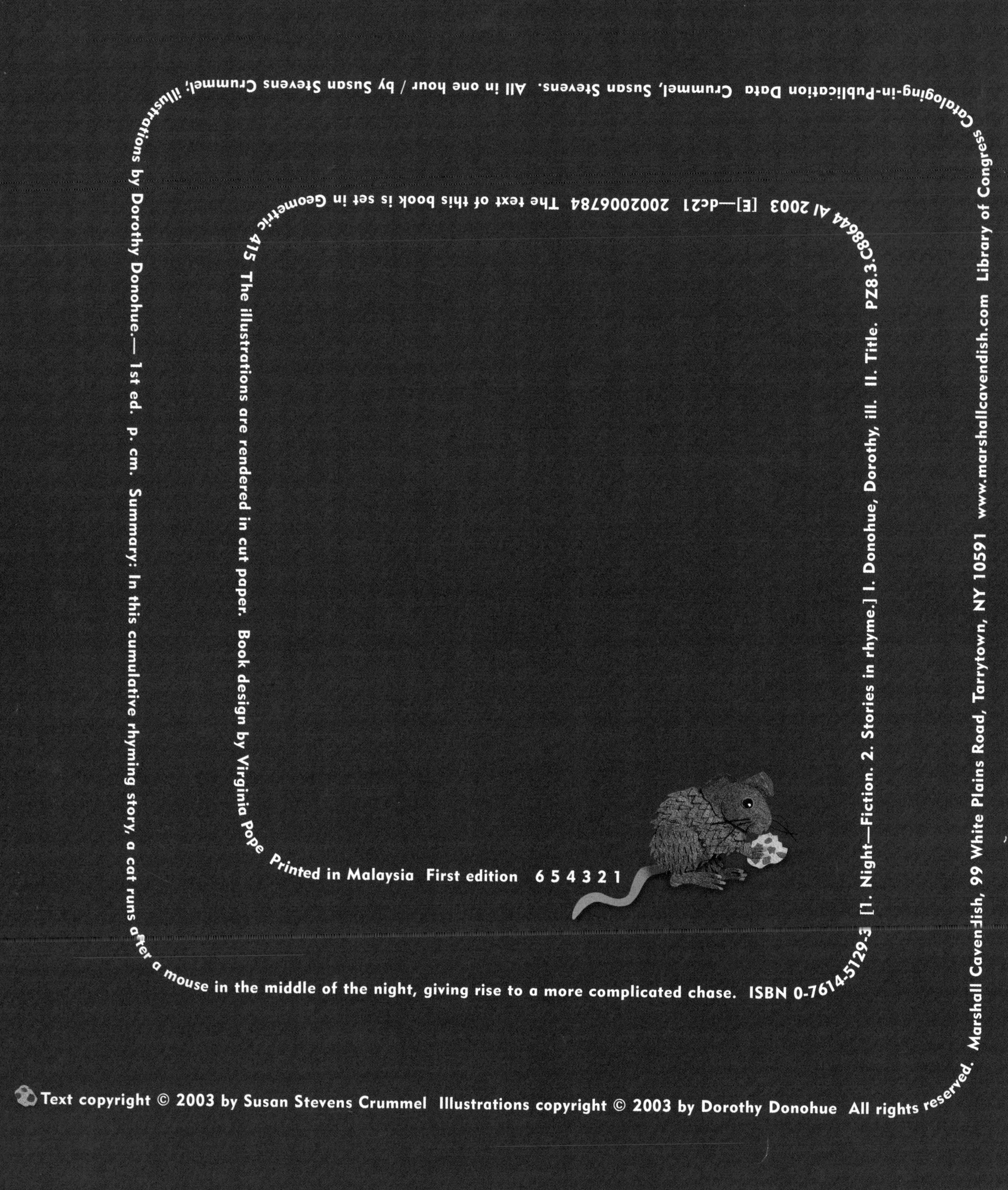

Text copyright © 2003 by Susan Stevens Crummel Illustrations copyright © 2003 by Dorothy Donohue All rights reserved.

Marshall Cavendish, 99 White Plains Road, Tarrytown, NY 10591 www.marshallcavendish.com

Library of Congress Cataloging-in-Publication Data Crummel, Susan Stevens. All in one hour / by Susan Stevens Crummel; illustrations by Dorothy Donohue.— 1st ed. p. cm. Summary: In this cumulative rhyming story, a cat runs after a mouse in the middle of the night, giving rise to a more complicated chase. ISBN 0-7614-5129-3 [1. Night—Fiction. 2. Stories in rhyme.] I. Donohue, Dorothy, ill. II. Title. PZ8.3.C88644 Al 2003 [E]—dc21 2002006784

The text of this book is set in Geometric 415 The illustrations are rendered in cut paper. Book design by Virginia Pope

Printed in Malaysia First edition 6 5 4 3 2 1

jj Fic